It was a sunny day, and Dora and Boots were playing hide-and-seek in the Flowery Garden.

"I found you!" shouted Dora, pointing up towards the tree.

"I've been caught!" giggled Boots.

Suddenly Dora stopped and listened. "Oh, no! I think I hear someone crying."

Dora and Boots followed the sound over to the teary Grumpy Old Troll.
"Hi, Mr Troll," said Dora. "Is something wrong?"

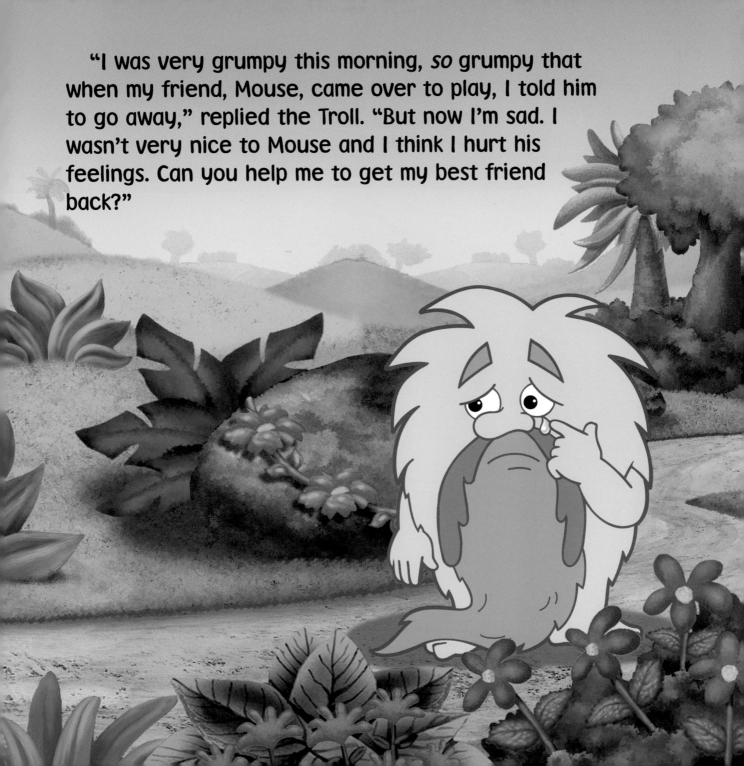

"I was very grumpy this morning, *so* grumpy that when my friend, Mouse, came over to play, I told him to go away," replied the Troll. "But now I'm sad. I wasn't very nice to Mouse and I think I hurt his feelings. Can you help me to get my best friend back?"

"We can help you, Mr Troll," replied Dora.

"Great!" said the Troll. "I know some riddles about being nice. Will you help me answer them?"

"Sure! We love riddles!" exclaimed Boots.

"All right, here's my first riddle," said the Troll.

"It was wrong to be grumpy to Mouse. I was very bad. What's the nice thing to say, so my friend won't be mad?"

"That's a great idea! I'll tell Mouse that I'm sorry!" cried the Grumpy Old Troll. "But I don't know where Mouse is," he continued sadly.

"We can check the Map," said Dora. "Say 'Map!'"

"I know how to find Mouse," said Map. "Mouse ran all the way back to his house. So you'll have to cross Sneezing Snake Lake, then go over Dragon Mountain, and that's how you'll get to Mouse's House."

Soon Dora, Boots, and the Troll arrived at the edge of Sneezing Snake Lake.

"How will we get across the lake?" wondered Boots.

Suddenly the Troll said,

"Look! It's Tico! And he's coming our way.
But how should I greet him? What's the nice thing to say?"

"Please, dragons, will you move out of the way?" the Troll called.

"We're sorry!" the dragons replied. "We didn't mean to block the road. We just wanted some ice cream! Please? *¿Por favor?*"

"Sure!" said Val, and she handed everyone an ice-cream cone.

When they reached the top of Dragon Mountain, suddenly dragons jumped out and blocked the road.

"GO AWAY!" shouted the Troll.

But the dragons wouldn't budge.

"Hmm," said the Troll.

"Shouting won't scare these dragons away.
If I want them to move, what's the nice thing to say?"

The Troll saw an ice-cream van driving up the road.

"Look! Our friend Val the octopus is driving that ice-cream van. I bet she can take us over Dragon Mountain," Dora said.

"I remember what to do," said the Troll, and he called out, "*¡Hola!* Hello, Val!"

Val stopped the ice-cream van, and they all climbed inside.

"Where do we go next?" asked Boots.

"I know!" said the Troll. "We have to go over Dragon Mountain."

"Can you see anything that will take us over Dragon Mountain?" asked Boots.

"¡*Gracias,* Tico!" called the Troll.
"¡*De nada!*" Tico replied as he sailed away.

Once they landed at the dock Dora, Boots, and the Troll jumped out of the boat.
The Troll said,

"Tico got us across the lake lickety-split! How do we let him know we appreciate it?"

Tico sailed the boat around all the sneezing snakes.

They all put on life jackets and climbed aboard. Suddenly sneezing snakes started popping up!

"Achoo! Achoo!" sneezed the snakes.

"Oh, no!" said the Troll. "All this sneezing is making my nose tickle. I think I'm going to sneeze.

*"I could sure use some more advice from you.
When I have to sneeze, what should I do?"*

"Hello! ¡*Hola*, Tico!" waved the Troll.
Tico offered to take Dora, Boots, and the
Troll across Sneezing Snake Lake in his boat.

Suddenly they heard a rustle coming from above.

"Look, it's Swiper! He's going to try and swipe our ice cream," said Boots.

"We have to stop Swiper," said Dora. "Say 'Swiper, no swiping!'"

"Oh Mannn!" said Swiper as he flew away.

"Hmmm," said the Troll, "I've just learnt something:

Swiping is not a nice thing to do.

If Swiper asked nicely, he could have ice cream too!"

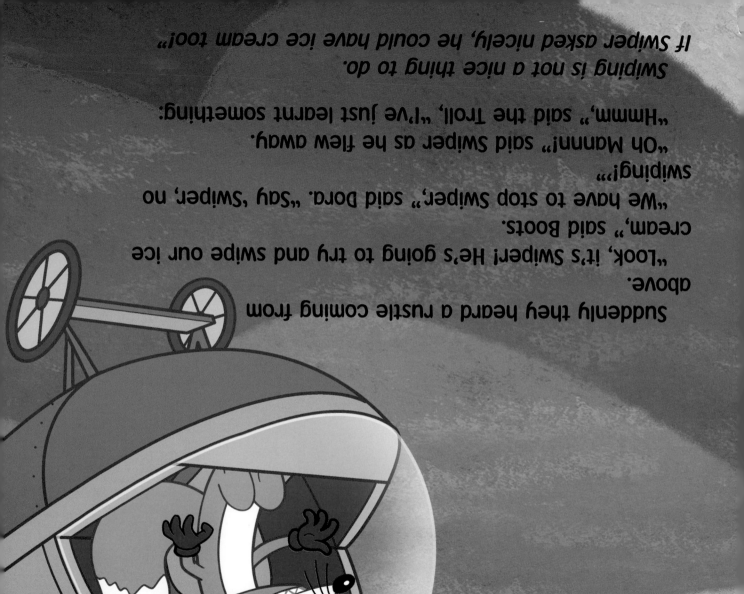

Soon Dora, Boots, and the Troll arrived at Mouse's House. The Troll knocked on the door.
"Mouse, please come out. I want to apologise," said the Troll.

Mouse opened the door and the Troll said, "I'm sorry I was grumpy. I was not a nice friend. Will you forgive me? Please? *¿Por favor?*"

Mouse was so happy to see the Troll that he said, "Yes! I forgive you!"

"Thank you! *¡Gracias!*" said the Troll.

"Hooray!" cheered Dora and Boots. "Mouse and the Troll are friends again! We did it!"

The Troll was so glad to play with his friends! He danced a happy dance as he said,

"*I learned many things on our trip.*
You have to be nice if you want friendship.
Friends are helpful and caring and go out of their way.
So I'll be kind and polite – at least for today!"